Fjords

Great Barrier Reef

Mt. Everest

Ayers Rock

Icebergs

Ladybird FIRST FACTS ABOUT™
THE EARTH

By Caroline Arnold
Illustrated by Meryl Henderson

Ladybird Books

Where do you live?

Near an ocean, lake, or river?
High in the mountains?
In the middle of a forest or desert?

People live in many different kinds of places. But we all live on the planet Earth.

If you took a trip to outer space, you could see the whole earth. It would look like a giant blue ball spinning in space.

The earth is huge. It would take 25 million people holding hands to make one circle around the earth!

5

Most of us cannot travel to outer space. But we can look at a globe. A globe is a model of the earth.

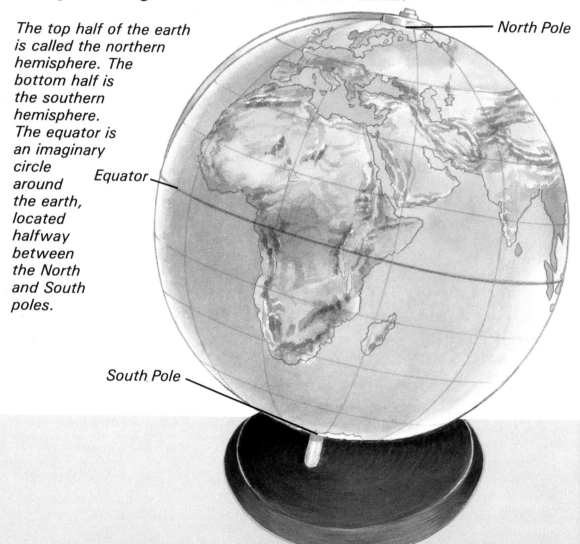

The top half of the earth is called the northern hemisphere. The bottom half is the southern hemisphere. The equator is an imaginary circle around the earth, located halfway between the North and South poles.

North Pole

Equator

South Pole

The biggest land masses on earth are the seven continents. They are North America, South America, Europe, Asia, Africa, Australia, and Antarctica.

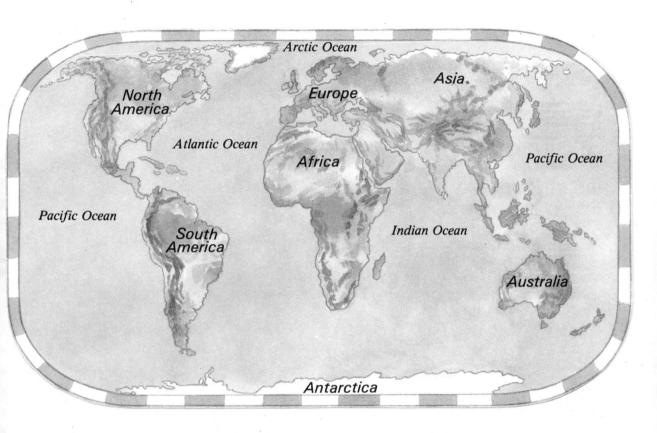

Which continent do you live on?

The surface of the earth is made up of land and water.

An *island* is a piece of land completely surrounded by water.

The Statue of Liberty is on an island in New York Harbor.

A *peninsula* is a piece of land that has water on three sides.

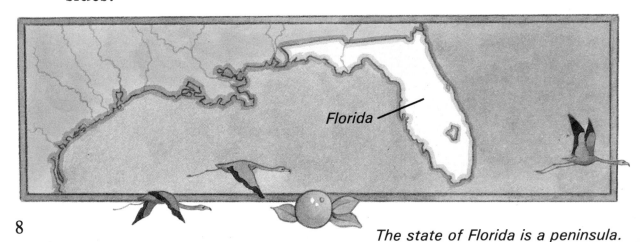

Florida

The state of Florida is a peninsula.

An *isthmus* joins two larger pieces of land.

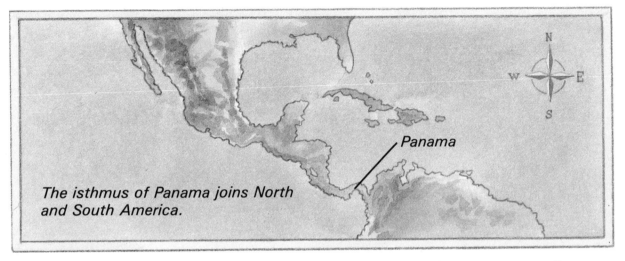

Panama

The isthmus of Panama joins North and South America.

Sometimes land partly surrounds a body of water to make a *bay*.

San Francisco Bay is a safe harbor for ships.

The surface of the globe is smooth. But the surface of the real earth has many bumps and ridges.

Some of the earth's land forms tall mountains.

The highest mountains in the world are the Himalayas in Tibet. They are over five miles high.

Like many valleys, the Tennessee Valley was formed by rushing river water.

In other places there are deep valleys and canyons.

It's fun to hike to the top of a hill to get a good view.

But much of the earth's land is mostly flat or has gently rolling hills.

The broad plains of the midwestern United States are good for growing crops and raising animals.

What is the land like where you live?

About two-thirds of the earth is covered with water.

We use water for transportation, for energy, to water crops, for drinking, and for fun.

Almost all of the earth's water is in oceans and seas. Yet we cannot drink sea water because it is too salty. Instead we use fresh water from lakes, rivers, and underground wells.

Water from the Colorado River is stored in a reservoir behind the Hoover Dam.

When we dig holes in the ground, we can find water in the earth.

Water changes the land we live on.

Ocean waves break up rocks along the shore and turn them into sand.

Gentle rains dissolve minerals in the soil and help plants to grow.

We could not live without water. We use it every day.

Rivers and waterfalls carve out valleys and canyons.

When water freezes it expands and can make cracks in rocks and soil.

One of the most important parts of our planet is invisible —its atmosphere.

The atmosphere is like a blanket around the earth.
It traps the sun's heat and helps keep us warm.

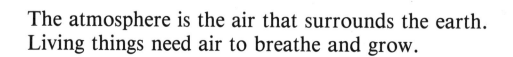

The atmosphere is the air that surrounds the earth. Living things need air to breathe and grow.

Every place on earth has its own climate.

In some places it rains a lot. In others it is mostly dry. The temperature varies from place to place too. Most people prefer to live where it is not too hot and not too cold.

The surface of the earth is made of rocks, sand, and soil. This is the earth's crust. But if you could cut the earth open, you would find melted rock inside.

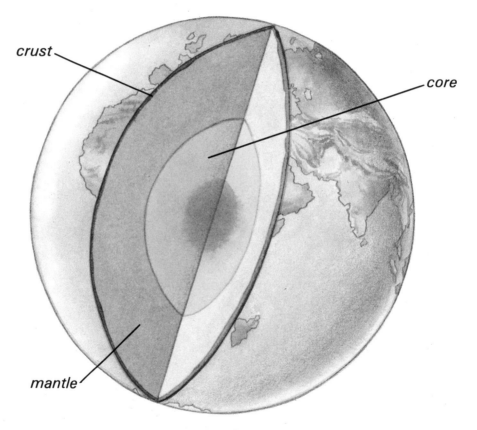

crust

core

mantle

The center of the earth is about 4,000 miles from the surface. No one can go there because it is too hot.

Pieces of the earth's crust slide across the melted rock underneath. When a part moves suddenly, we have an earthquake.

Sometimes a hole in the earth's crust allows melted rock to come up from below. Then we have a volcano.

People who study the earth are called geologists. They think that the earth was formed about four and half billion years ago. Since then it has slowly changed from a rocky landscape to a living planet.

*4½ billion years ago.
The earth is formed.*

*500 million years ago.
Early forms of life live in warm seas.*

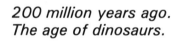

*200 million years ago.
The age of dinosaurs.*

Scientists believe that modern people first lived on the earth about 35,000 years ago.

In places like the Grand Canyon in Arizona, you can find clues to some of the earth's history. There, over millions of years, the Colorado River has cut through many layers of rock. The newest rocks are at the top of the canyon walls. The oldest ones are near the bottom.

Geologists can figure out how old a rock is by finding out what it is made of and where it was found.

basalt *granite*

Some rocks are formed when melted rock from inside the earth cools off and hardens. They are called igneous rocks. Basalt and granite are igneous rocks.

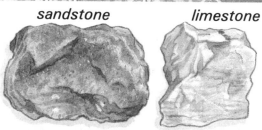

sandstone *limestone*

Some rocks are formed from matter that collects and hardens on the bottoms of lakes and rivers. They are called sedimentary rocks. Sandstone and limestone are sedimentary rocks

You can collect rocks where you live and find out what they are.

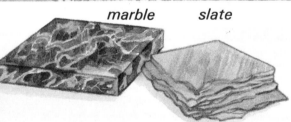

marble   slate

trilobite fossil

Rocks that have been changed in some way are called metamorphic rocks. Marble and slate are metamorphic rocks.

Fossils are remains of plants and animals that have been preserved in some way. Limestone often contains fossils of ancient sea creatures.

23

Rocks and minerals are part of the earth's natural resources. We use natural resources every day.

We use rocks such as granite and marble to construct buildings.

Some rocks contain metal. We use iron ore to make steel for machinery.

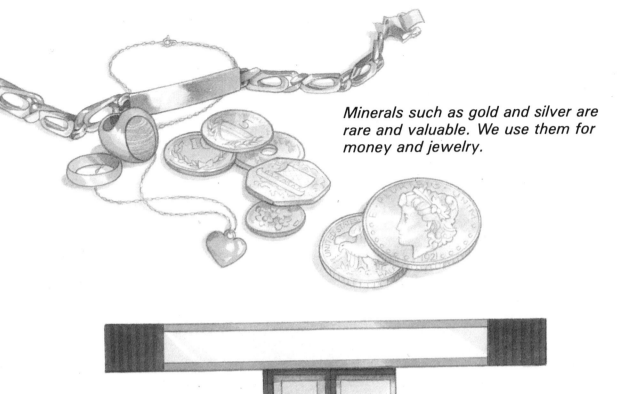

Minerals such as gold and silver are rare and valuable. We use them for money and jewelry.

We burn coal, gas, and oil for energy.

25

The earth provides us with everything we need. It gives us air to breathe, water to drink, food to eat, places to live, and sources of energy. We must take care of the earth well to preserve it for the future.

GLOSSARY

atmosphere   the air surrounding the earth

continent   one of the main land masses on earth

earthquake   sudden movement of the earth's crust

equator   an imaginary circle around the earth, located halfway between the North and South poles

fossil   the preserved remains of a plant or animal

geologist   a person who studies the earth's structure and history, and how it changes

globe   a model of the earth

island   a piece of land that is completely surrounded by water

isthmus   a narrow piece of land that connects two larger land masses

North Pole   the most northerly point on earth

northern hemisphere   all of the earth north of the equator

peninsula   land that is surrounded by water on three sides

South Pole   the most southerly point on earth

southern hemisphere   all of the earth south of the equator

volcano   an opening in the earth's crust, through which smoke, lava (melted rock), and ash escape